Tom is sitting at the top of the big hill with his bin lid. He is waiting for Bella.

Bella is coming up the hill with her bin lid. She puffs and pants as she climbs up to the top.

At last she gets to the top. She sits down next to Tom. 'I need a rest,' she says.

'Do you want to go down the hill first,' says Tom. Bella sits on her bin lid.

Tom gives Bella a big push and off she goes. She whizzes down the hill. 'Wheeee....,' she cries.

Then Tom sits on his bin lid. He pushes with his hands and his feet but he hardly moves.

Oh no! Tom's bin lid is stuck in the sand. He gets off his lid and he rolls down the hill.

'Wow, that was fantastic,' he says to Bella. 'Let's climb to the top of the hill again.'